To Margaret Anastas & Kirsten Hall.
You two are the coolest of the cool.
—J.J. & P.O.

The Cool Bean
Text copyright © 2019 by Jory John
Illustrations copyright © 2019 by Pete Oswald
For information address HarperCollins Children's Books,
a division of HarperCollins Publishers, 195 Broadway, New York, NY 10007.
www.harpercollinschildrens.com
ISBN 978-0-06-295452-7
The artist used scanned watercolor textures
and digital paint to create the illustrations for this book.
Typography by Jeanne L. Hogle
20 21 22 23 PC 10 9 8 7 6 5 4 3
❖
First Edition

THE COOL BEAN

written by Jory John • illustrations by Pete Oswald

HARPER
An Imprint of HarperCollinsPublishers

WATCH OUT!

Here come the cool beans!

The *coooooool* beans.

Oh yeah . . . check out how they move.

Look at the way they swagger.

Notice their sunglasses. **Yow!**

The cool beans are known all over school.
From house to house.
Across town.
Beyond county lines.

In the olden days, last year,
we were all one big pod of beans.
We were a mixed bag, but
somehow it worked.

Yep. Those were the good old days...

and then we stopped seeing each other as much.

That's just how it is sometimes. You spend
less time together, even though you're not
totally sure why.

I watched as the beans I knew so well—the beans from my own pod—became the cool beans.

Oh, they were *soooooo cooooool.*

One of them could play the guitar. **COOL**.

One of them could draw the best superheroes. **COOOOOOL**.

One of them could jump higher than any bean I'd ever known. **COOOOOOOOOL**.

ME?

Well, I mostly stayed the same.

Sure, I made some *small* changes.

I wore sunglasses.

"Too big."

I was still picked last for everything.

My clothes never seemed to fit.

"HONK!"

I snorted when I laughed.

"WHUMP!"

I walked into stuff.

I was an *uncool* bean, for sure.

I started thinking of myself as just
a common bean with no special skills.
I couldn't compete, so I didn't even try.

I'd *never* be a cool bean.

It seemed like there were two types of beans in the world.

There were the cool beans...

and the beans like me.

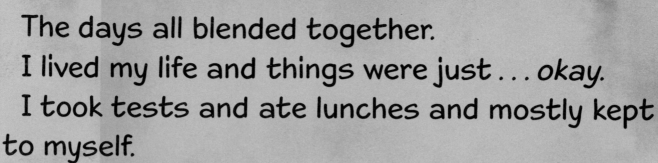

The days all blended together.
I lived my life and things were just ... *okay*.
I took tests and ate lunches and mostly kept
to myself.

The cool beans continued being cool.

I mean, sure, I missed them. A bit.
But it's not like I was going to *say* anything.
I felt like all that coolness had gotten in
the way of our friendship.

And that's how it went...
until one day.

I was in the cafeteria. I dropped my lunch on my loafers.

But then something sort of miraculous happened.

Out of nowhere, one of the cool beans helped me clean it up. He didn't even say anything. He just gave me a nod. That was it.

Later, I was out on the playground. I tripped and scraped my knee and maybe cried a little bit and everybody saw it.

Another one of the cool beans came to my side...

and, without a word, he dusted me off.

That afternoon, I was sitting in class. I wasn't really paying attention.

I didn't notice, but our teacher had called on me. Everybody stared. I sat there in silence. Nobody said anything.

But then one of the cool beans stood up and came over to me. Everybody watched.

She leaned in close and whispered, "Hey. The teacher asked you to read from page 32." Then she gave me a quick wink and went back to her seat.

It was a small gesture, sure...

The GREAT GATSBEAN

but it was also *everything.*

I walked home with a goofy smile on my face.

I smiled all the way through dinner.

That day made all the difference.
It was a day that could've been really bad,
if not for the kindness of a few cool beans.

It gave me a shred of confidence. That shred
of confidence has continued to grow.

Somebody had my back.

Or . . . a *few* somebodies.

After that, I started hanging out with the cool beans again.

Not all the time.
But sometimes.

At lunch.

After school.

Even on the weekends.

Throughout all of this, I realized that it's not about how you look or any of that other silly stuff.

It's about a wink or a nod or a smile at just the right moment.

It's about dusting somebody off, helping them up again, and pointing them in the right direction.

"You need a hand?"

"Yes, please."

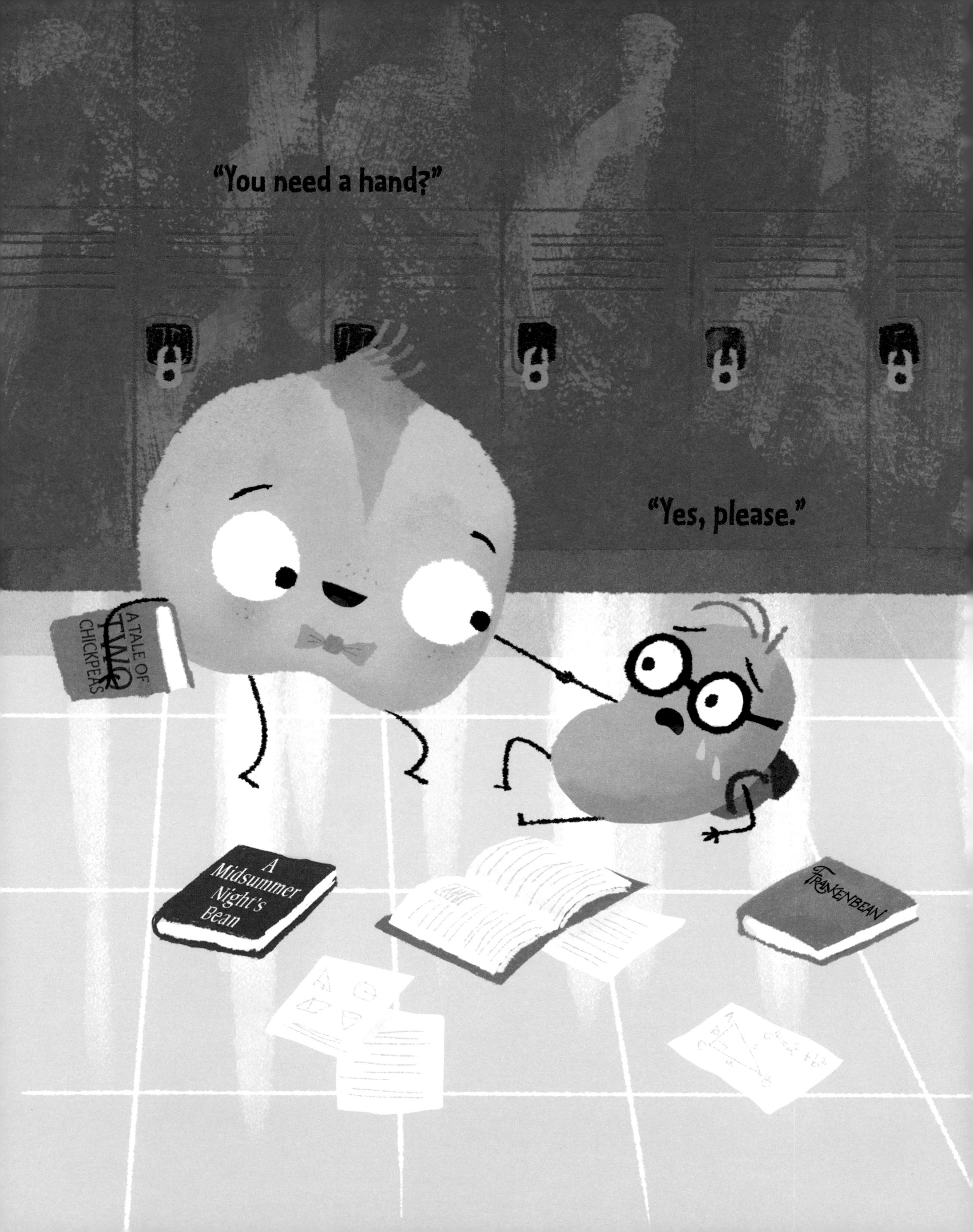

Now *that's* cool.